Anyone's Love Story

by Daniela Bayer

Copyright © 2010 Daniela Bayer
All rights reserved.

ISBN: 1449927912
ISBN-13: 9781449927912
LCCN: 2009913312

Contents

PART I
Falling pg. 1

Part II
Searching pg. 25

Part III
Accepting pg. 47

Part IV
Knowing pg. 75

Part V
Loving pg. 93

Part VI
Having pg. 121

Part VII
Understanding pg. 141

*To my Love
forever and always.*

My heart speaks to me, but no one can hear its words.
It is then, when I am receiving these silent messages,
that I take a pen, open my book, and write on paper
what my heart wants me to record.

It is only when I start speaking that
the noise of my voice interferes with the silence within me,
and the fragile communication lines break down.

And my heart continues only to count my time.

When silence is restored,
my heart surrenders to it and speaks in a silently loud voice.

And I pick up a pen again and continue writing
the unfolding story of my heart.

PART I
Falling

Anyone's Love Story

Falling

This is the day I fell down from Cloud Nine

and landed firmly on my feet.

I think I am on my own again.

I have to be strong.
I will make it work for me again.
It is like the wind of change
swirled around me again.
It is time to move on; my life is changing.

Time for growth.
I am not allowed to backslide.
I have to move forward
at full speed.

Anyone's Love Story

Falling

I am sitting on the top stair
overlooking the living room,
looking at the walls, windows,
the picture on the wall,
the candleholders,
the TV, radio, couch, the plants,
the curtains, the ceiling light ...

Thinking.

And remembering.

We had a good life.

Time to move on.

And have another
good life.

Anyone's Love Story

Falling

I don't like the past.

I want the new
and I don't know what the new is
or how to let go of the old.

Anyone's Love Story

Falling

It is so sad to watch the dying of love.

I know exactly when it is happening.

I feel the pain

and the resignation.

The emptiness.

Anyone's Love Story

Falling

I am hurting ... quietly, slowly,

painfully.

The love I thought I would have with you

was nothing but a fantasy.

Painful years filled with laughter, adventure, loving acts,

holding hands, kissing, hugging.

For the moment.

Gosh, honest men are hard to come by.

Anyone's Love Story

Falling

So many missed opportunities for kindness, caring,

compassion.

So many,

too many!

missed opportunities to stand by each other,

to stand up and let the whole world know

that we are together,

bulletproof, strong, dedicated,

impenetrable,

the best of friends, lovers, partners,

husband and wife.

A unit, one, together.

Anyone's Love Story

Falling

I did everything

I could.

And so I have peace

within me.

Anyone's Love Story

Falling

There comes a point
when saving myself
is more important than
other people's agendas.

Anyone's Love Story

Falling

There comes a morning

when I wake up and realize that

the cost of fighting for what I think I am entitled to

is far greater than

the cost of letting go of everything.

And I take in a nice, long, deep breath

and I release my grip on the past

and I say hello

to my

future.

Anyone's Love Story

Falling

I think this is the first time
in my life that
I understand and realize
the power of choice.

The power of *my* choice.

Anyone's Love Story

Falling

It is possible to heal.

PART II
Searching

Anyone's Love Story

Searching

You wanted me changed.
You wanted me
to look the other way.

And I did.
And I discovered opportunities for myself
when I looked to new horizons.

I saw my life in the distance.
And I turned to take a better look
and to explore.

And I went the other way too.

Anyone's Love Story

Searching

Who am I?

How far will I go?

Where do I draw the line?

At what point do I stop and turn around?

When do I snap back?

What do I want?

What do I need?

What do I desire?

What do I must have?

When do I say "enough"!

How do I say "enough"?

When do I leave?

Where do I go …

and with whom?

Anyone's Love Story

Searching

One last time

I am turning back
to make sure that
I haven't forgotten anything.

To make sure that
I can live with my consciousness
and knowing that

I did everything I could.

Anyone's Love Story

Searching

I am too far out without you
and you scream now
and you try to pull me back.

I cannot go back.
I have changed.

I know what I want.

I know what it looks like
and I know what it will feel like.

I know I deserve it.

I know I need to allow me to have it.

Anyone's Love Story

Searching

When I release

all my thoughts of you

and when I reach

that sacred space within me

that is

me

what do I feel?

Sheer joy.

Anyone's Love Story

Searching

I am choosing to redirect

my thinking and my feelings

and focus on positive

bright

happy

things.

Those things that lift me up

and bring joy

into my soul and spirit.

I am making a choice.

Forever.

Anyone's Love Story

Searching

I know who you are
and I don't hate you.

We are on separate paths.

I was sad, very sad back then
and I am happy now.
Not with you.

You be you and live your life.
And I will live mine.
All is well.

I numbed the pain and there is no going back for me.

Peace.

Anyone's Love Story

Searching

I see your name on an e-mail that just arrived.

I look at the name

and I know it looks familiar.

I know I should have some kind of emotion and response

within me.

I check with myself

consciously

and I feel

nothing.

There is the feeling of nothingness.

The same as if I were looking at a picture of the

surface of the moon.

I have seen the picture many times before.

Seeing it again, well

I know the moon is there

and it has a purpose.

And I can go about my life

and I don't have to do anything about it.

I don't even have to think about it.

Anyone's Love Story

Searching

I know

I am on the right path.

I know

I am doing the right thing.

I am sorry

that I endured so much drama over the years.

I no longer have the need

to be

a victim.

Anyone's Love Story

Searching

Something great is beginning for me.

It feels like I am shedding the old skin

to show the

new, fresh, radiant, happy, content

me.

When I am done with this process

I will not look back.

This was a harsh lesson for me.

Very painful.

A life-changing experience.

I changed as a result of it.

Some things,

many I hope,

changed for the better.

Some things

changed for the worse.

I have a long road ahead of me to overcome these.

I know

I make things happen.

PART III
Accepting

Anyone's Love Story

Accepting

Relationships, like everything else in life,
have their purpose and time.

Relationships die
and that is okay.

We change
and some things have to go
as we shed the old skin.

Anyone's Love Story

Accepting

I feel like I am standing here

in a new baby skin,

white and soft.

I feel like a newborn.

With a new

great life

ahead of me.

Anyone's Love Story

Accepting

I keep putting one foot in front of the other

and before I know it

I am miles away

from where I started.

Anyone's Love Story

Accepting

I left everything behind
and took myself
on this incredible journey.

I conquered.
I reached.
I tore walls down.
I achieved.

I failed
and I picked myself up
and continued marching forward.

Anyone's Love Story

Accepting

All is well.

Really.

All is well.

I let go of all attachments.
I let go of all expectations
and place myself into the now.

Here and *now*.

I choose to be a hero
in my own life story.

Anyone's Love Story

Accepting

I cherish myself

and the uniqueness and goodness of my soul.

I know

I always have a choice.

I also know now that

I don't have to make the choice

today or tomorrow.

Anyone's Love Story

Accepting

I make the choice when

I am ready.

I make the choice when

I have done enough work

to know.

Yes.

Now make the choice.

The choice is always mine to make.

Anyone's Love Story

Accepting

I really am the only one
who can define for myself
what is important to me.

Anyone's Love Story

Accepting

I feel like

I just came back

from wherever I was.

I feel like me again.

Anyone's Love Story

Accepting

I dip my toe into the stream of life

and I like it.

That is where I am today.

I know what I want.

Anyone's Love Story

Accepting

I am stepping up and stepping out
to get what I desire.

And I want the best.

I am ready to claim it.
I am so ready to enjoy it.
I want it in my life.
And it will come to me.

I know.

Anyone's Love Story

Accepting

I love myself and I love my life.

I am so proud of who I am

and who I am becoming.

I don't feel compelled to rush things

or do things that I am not ready to do.

I am in sync with the flow of life

and I am the river.

I let myself go

wherever I desire to take me.

What an exquisite journey.

How fun.

Anyone's Love Story

Accepting

I have waited for this moment
my whole life.

I have learned my lessons.
I know my limitations
and I celebrate my successes.

I am no more the shy, insecure Cinderella.

I am genuinely happy
and I love my place in the sun.
I had to work through a lot of *heavy* stuff
and this was the way to do it.

It doesn't matter how long it took.
I am finally here!

PART IV

Knowing

Anyone's Love Story

Knowing

Love is all around me

and I am learning to pay attention to it.

I am learning

to allow my heart

to plunge into the warm feeling.

I am learning

to let go

and enjoy the beauty and love that

I am surrounded by.

I am learning

to allow my soul

to respond to the feeling.

I am learning to recognize all of these.

I am learning

to love

and

to let love

come to me.

Anyone's Love Story

Knowing

I am worth loving.

Anyone's Love Story

Knowing

I want a man in my life

who wants me as much as I want him.

I want someone who loves me

with all his heart and soul.

Someone who believes in

having a good life.

Someone who I am comfortable being with

and being around.

Someone who I can be proud to be with.

Someone who is happy.

The love of my life.

Forever and always.

Anyone's Love Story

Knowing

I want to like what I am looking at.

I want to admire his brain.

I want to love his heart.

I want to respect the choices he has made.

I want to have fun with him

doing many different things.

I want to feel safe and secure

in a beautiful home with a garden

filled with love.

Anyone's Love Story

Knowing

Over the last couple of nights
I had a very special dream.

I woke up in the middle of the night
with complete clarity of mind.

I have been in love with you forever.

It has been such a long time …
I wonder if you know what I feel.

You have claimed a very special place in my heart.

Each time I think about you
I feel embraced
by love.

Anyone's Love Story

Knowing

I don't know
if there is a soul mate
for every person
in every lifetime.

The realization that
I met my soul mate
in this lifetime
is a bit overwhelming
and incredibly touching.

Anyone's Love Story

Knowing

After running around
and learning my lessons in life,
falling on my knees
and rising to the sun,
I have finally realized that
what I am looking for
I already found.

What I am looking for
has been in my life for a very long time.

It is a beautiful feeling to know.

Anyone's Love Story

Knowing

I realized that after all these years

you

still have a very special place in my heart.

I realized that

you

are

the

Love of my Life.

PART V

Loving

Anyone's Love Story

Loving

Never doubt love.

Love is real.

Always.

Anyone's Love Story

Loving

There is not and there has never been anyone else
who makes me feel this way.

There is no one else
who I think about
so much.

No one else
has made my heart sing
so consistently
over the years.

All our moments together
are as alive today
as they were years ago.

I can still feel the gentle touch of your hand.
The light kiss you planted in my hair.
I still feel your energy.

And I have butterflies in my stomach
every time I think about you.

Loving

I love you.

I die to tell you.

I know I am late.

I wish I were better prepared then
and better able to know my truth.

There was a lot of clutter in my world.

We met too soon.

Anyone's Love Story

Loving

There might have been a time when
I blamed myself
for not grabbing the opportunity.

In retrospect I know.
There can't be any talk of my missing the boat.

I was not ready.

Anyone's Love Story

Loving

There might have been a time when
I could not forgive myself.

What I said and what I did not say.
What I should have said, and when.

A part of me says, oh well …

Then another part of me thinks that
I could have done better.

Today I know

I did the best I could.

Anyone's Love Story

Loving

I want you to know that

I finally got it.

I have no idea if I will ever have the opportunity to tell you.
And so I am sending these loving thoughts to you
and I wish that

you receive them.

Anyone's Love Story

Loving

Let go.

Anyone's Love Story

Loving

Here I am.

Another end
and another new beginning.

Spiraling upward
closer and closer to the stars.

Ascending.
Knowing love.
Feeling self-love.

Always wiser, always knowing.

Loving

Life is like the sea.

It isn't trying to make waves
and bring treasures to my feet.

It simply does.

Anyone's Love Story

Loving

I sit on a beach

and watch the waves come in

and I wonder …

What is Love?

Love is a bouquet.

A bouquet of flowers.

A sweet scent.

What else do I need to know?

Flowers bloom everywhere.

Anyone's Love Story

Loving

Keep your heart open.

Be without judgment.

Have no fear.

Believe in a fairytale ending.

Anyone's Love Story

Loving

Hold the image of greatness

you saw in him

when you first met.

You will meet again

as if for the first time.

Anyone's Love Story

Loving

Love?

Intrigue.

Passion?

Desire.

Conquer?

Reach.

Have?

Hold.

See?

Touch.

Smell?

Taste.

Mine. Yours?

Now.

What will be?

You. Me.

PART VI
Having

Anyone's Love Story

Having

Writing about my desires,
I know that I am already there.

I have it.
I have all of it.

All I have to do is open the door
and let it all come to me.

I am where I need to be.
Things are the way they are supposed to be.

Anyone's Love Story

Having

I don't have to ask you to come to me.

You come automatically because
here is where you want to be.

And you are free to act on that desire.

Anyone's Love Story

Having

I stand here

ready to embrace what life has to offer

for the rest of my days on this planet

and forever and ever into eternity.

The real love.

The true love.

The love that is gentle and warm and soothing and healing.

The kind that always has been there for me.

I am finally ready to have it.

I am ready to feel it.

I am ready to experience it in my life

and in my being.

I appreciate its patience.

That it never gave up,

always hopeful that

one day

I would open my eyes and see it.

Anyone's Love Story

Having

Sitting under a big tree,

basking in the glowing light,

the gentle summer breeze,

and a bird's song.

Ah, and the sweet scent of a flower in my hand.

Anyone's Love Story

Having

I run my fingers through your hair
and love feels like sunshine to me.
It warms my heart
and puts a smile on my face.

I want to be with you
because being with you
feels so good to me.

I can be myself.

Anyone's Love Story

Having

I let my light shine
and I stand with my arms wide open.
My face is lit with all my beauty
and the rays of light of the sun.

I am smiling with my mouth and eyes,
holding the deep love in my heart
and the deepest understanding in my soul.

How did all this happen?

It started with a dream.

Anyone's Love Story

Having

I have feelings that I have never had before.
I am receiving love like I have never received love before.
The iceberg inside of me has started to melt.

I feel my heart warming up
and this feeling flows through my whole body.
Suddenly I am aware of myself in a whole new way.

My heart sings.

Anyone's Love Story

Having

When you speak to me
it is like music
coming to my ears
and sinking into my heart.

I feel so immersed
in the sea of love, caring, and gentleness
that tears rush into my eyes
and I don't stop them.
I allow them to flow freely
and mingle with the salty waters around me.

Our love is like the sea
forever moving
between the dreams
of our souls.

Anyone's Love Story

Having

I am finally home.

My love.

Forever and always.

PART VII
Understanding

Anyone's Love Story

Understanding

I chose this life because
I wanted to experience
what it would be like

to be

me.

Anyone's Love Story

Understanding

I am a writer

I run a business

I am a friend

I am somebody's daughter

I love dogs

I am a neighbor

I am a customer

I am a traveler

I am a passionate lover

I don't know how to cook

I am a role model

I am a teacher

I am a student

I am a human being,
full of my own inhibitions
and perfect in every way.

Anyone's Love Story

Understanding

I give myself permission
to set boundaries that
feel true and comfortable.

I don't need to make anything up.

I am vulnerable and powerful
at the same time.

I am genuine and perfect
in my own imperfect way.

Anyone's Love Story

Understanding

I walk my path

knowing all too well

that this truly is

my own chosen path.

I follow my heart

and listen to my exquisite intuition.

I am a magician.

I create my own reality.

And I line up people and events and circumstances

to greet me

at the right moment

when I seek and find

the fruit of my own enlightenment

and receive

the gift of knowing.

Anyone's Love Story

Understanding

I know

some questions have no easy answers.

They are simple questions.

They are not easy.

When I look up the word "simple"

in the thesaurus

it says "easy."

But it is not the same.

Sometimes

what is simple

can be plain difficult.

Anyone's Love Story

Understanding

At any moment
the ghosts may surprise me.

I can't go back
and rewrite the past, but
I can rewrite my understanding of it.
The players are the same
as I rewrite their characters and roles.

And I may just find that
the players I hated most,
the ones who hurt me the most,
the ones who I ran away from

were indeed the ones
from whom I learned

the most.

Anyone's Love Story

Understanding

In a strange way

I start appreciating them because

I know

they helped me uncover my beauty.

They may not have seen my beauty.

Hell, they may not even have acknowledged

the possibility of my beauty.

Neither may I have admitted

their beauty to myself.

It doesn't matter.

I uncovered beauty

as a result of their and my

ugliness.

Anyone's Love Story

Understanding

No sense in wallowing in the pain of what was,

sacrificing each present moment

for the purpose of the past.

I stop

as soon as I understand

what is happening.

I stop

as soon as

I realize that

I

am

the

answer.

Anyone's Love Story

Understanding

Sometimes life brings me
to the edge of a cliff
and says,

Jump. Close your eyes if you need to.

And I jump.
Going on blind faith.

Always landing safely.

Anyone's Love Story

Understanding

Life is one big sequence of trial and error and success.

Life is a mysterious and beautiful collage
of sparkle and color and taste and touch and feeling.

And I always reach for the best karmic link.

It is all here for me
ready for the sampling.

It is all here for me
ready for the tasting.

It is all here for me
ready for the taking.

Anyone's Love Story

Understanding

I keep an open mind

and allow myself to be surprised.

Sometimes

what looks like a wet blanket

turns into a magic carpet

right in front of my eyes.

Anyone's Love Story

Understanding

Didn't I know all this?
I must have forgotten.

It is my pleasure to remind myself.

All the guidance I am seeking
I already have at my disposal.

Anyone's Love Story

Understanding

Bite the bullet.

Anyone's Love Story

Understanding

Trust the process of life.

Anyone's Love Story

Understanding

Love is an adventure.

Made in the USA
Charleston, SC
09 June 2011